*Lost Love: My First Boyfriend*

# Lost Love: My First Boyfriend

## Nadia's Story

*By: Rachel Moulden*

eBook ISBN 978-1-945325-43-4

Paperback ISBN 978-1-945325-44-1

Cover illustration by Sarah Mensinga

Published by Ornamental Publishing LLC

# *Contents*

Staring out into the water while enjoying the serenity of the Detroit Riverwalk, I reminisced about the summer I had just experienced.

The fall season was approaching, and I already was missing what I loved most about summer. I missed its sunny days, warm weather, the fun festivals, and most of all, spending time with Aiden. Though we met through a summer art program and had just started to develop a deeper connection, soon everything fell apart toward summer's end.

School would be starting soon and I was trying to keep it together, but it was hard. Losing Aiden meant not only losing my boyfriend, but my best friend...

But I'm getting ahead of myself. Let's go back to the beginning of my story...

◆

LOST LOVE: MY FIRST BOYFRIEND

## CHAPTER ONE

A S THE summer vacation approached, I sat at my desk nervously tapping my foot anxiously awaiting three months of freedom from the drudgery of long school days. We were so close to summer vacation! I watched the clock as it ticked away second by second. Just a couple of more minutes and school would be over for the year!

My teacher tried to keep us focused while going over her standard end-of-the-school-year speech. You know...the typical "study over your summer vacation" and "do something meaningful with your free time" lecture that teachers always gave to students who are not paying attention (like me). We were obviously thinking of any and everything except whatever was being said.

I looked at the clock and my best friend Mia looked over at me with gleeful anticipation.

3.....2....1....Brrring! rang the sound of the final bell of the school year!

My entire classroom ran out with shouts and happy screams! Summer was finally here! Mia and I went down the hallway practically skipping with joy!

"Girl, I cannot wait to start the most epic summer ever!" said she.

"Me too," I stated, "I can't wait to hang out, try out all the newest restaurants, and go to a summer carnival."

Being the nerdy person that I am, I vowed that this was my summer to break out of my comfort zone and try something new. I was tired of being ordinary Nadia. And though my friends and family didn't think that I was boring, I felt like needed a change in my life. If I kept to myself and did the same things I usually did, how would I ever experience something new? How could I be more exciting and adventurous without losing who I was?

There's no doubt I would be in the library, nose deep inside a book, and catching up on all the reading I wanted to do while in school but didn't have the time to do. But this summer I wanted to try something different. But what? Summer camp wasn't really my thing, and I wasn't big into sports.

While running down a list of possible options, my thoughts were interrupted by my good friend Mia shouting from the school's entrance, "Nadia, are you coming? We don't have all day!"

As usual, our end of school year ritual was going to our local Athens Coney Island restaurant for some good food and going over a recap of the year.

"I'm coming," I said as I finished packing up my items from my locker and began racing to the door. I couldn't wait to see what this summer would bring!

Even though the Athens Coney Island was close to school we decided to take the bus. Though it was only a fifteen minute walk, the sun was blazing in the sky and it was an unusually hot day for the month of June. One thing I learned about living in Michigan was that its summer days typically tended to not get too sweltering until July rolled around. Obviously, Mother Nature had other plans in mind when it came to today's weather.

It was something about summer vacation that made me nostalgic for simple comfort foods. I pulled out my backpack and got out my art notebook. Covered in 90's anime stickers, looking at it brought me a feeling of security and comfort whenever I was feeling down. I loved taking it everywhere I went so I could draw what I saw, jot notes down about my day and anything else that came to mind. It was like a mixed media diary of sorts. I loved how I could journal and practice my art skills all in one notebook.

My dream job was to become an animator one day and work for one of the major animation studios but, for the moment, I was just happy with sketching whatever picture was sparked by my vivid imagination.

Once we arrived at the Coney Island, Mia and I ordered our favorite meal. A chocolate milkshake, fries, and a juicy double cheeseburger was our go-to summer treat. It wasn't the healthiest dish, but it was comfort food and who didn't like comfort food?

"So what's our plan for this summer?" I asked, "we have to finish our summer bucket list!"

I flipped through the pages of my notebook to find this year's summer bucket list and looked down at the page. So far we had:

1) Try two new food trucks
2) Eat a funnel cake at the local fair
3) Spend the day at Belle Isle
4) Visit the beach/water park
5) Play the latest *Animal Crossing* game
6) Have a horror movie marathon
7) Annual "I Spy" competition at Eastern Market

We didn't know if our parents had other plans for us this summer, but we were determined to accomplish as much of our list as possible and hopefully add in some new adventures as well. As per usual, I expected my parents to give me some dreaded summer task similar to last year's project of cleaning out the basement. Let me tell you, just thinking about our basement sends shudders down my spine. They were some pretty large cobwebs down there and I startled more than a few spiders that scrambled to find new homes once I managed to disturb their existing ones. I hoped and prayed that whatever this year's summer project was it had to be better this year. Right?

"So Nadia, I know we had planned on spending the entire summer together. But my parents and I are going on a trip to visit my grandparents in Florida for a month," said Mia. "When I come back, I'll be free to hang out with my bestie for the rest of the summer!"

"It's no problem!" I said. "I completely understand."

Mia's family hadn't been to see her grandparents in a while so I knew she was excited to go. Plus her family was coming together for a big family reunion. I was bummed, of course, but equally happy for my bestie.

After waiting for a while, our order finally came to the table and we immediately scarfed it all down. There was something about having a burger on a summer day that just reminded you of a classic outdoor barbeque. We chatted about the school year, gossiped about who had a crush on whom, and what we would expect next year. Come September, we'd be heading into 9th grade. We were excited, but a bit worried and nervous about what to expect entering high school.

As we finished our meals Mia texted her mom to come pick us up. We couldn't wait for the day that we could have our own set of wheels and didn't have to rely on our parents to take us places all the time. We usually walked a lot, but the Coney Island was somewhat far from our homes and taking the bus would take twice as long. After chatting while waiting for Mia's mom, about 20 minutes later she arrived.

"Hey girls!—What's shakin'?" said Mrs. Lopez.

I immediately laughed out loud. Her mom had such a vibrant spirit and always joked about keeping up with the kids in order to be more hip. Mia didn't say anything but I heard her let out an exasperated sigh under her breath to be dramatic. We hopped in the car and off we went.

"So did Mia tell you we're going away to Florida for part of the summer?" asked Mrs. Lopez, "I'd love to bring you along Nadia, but I wanted some family time for the summer before things get a bit hectic."

"It's no biggie, I completely understand," I replied.

We chatted all the way home about the upcoming summer and in no time I was at my house. Mia and I said our goodbyes, hugged, and I waved as they drove off. I hummed a little tune as I walked into the house and shut the door. I couldn't wait to see what this summer would bring!

"Nadia is that you?" mom shouted from somewhere in the house.

I walked toward the direction of her voice after setting my bag and shoes by the door. The smell of her cinnamon chocolate chip cookies led me to the kitchen.

"Hey mom!" I said while smiling at the remnants of cookie dough and flour all over the counter and her shirt.

I couldn't help but giggle. She even had of couple of pieces in her dark wavy hair, and the flour on her skin made her look like a ghost! My mom loved to bake! Like drawing and sketching relaxed me, baking was my mom's saving grace. She never saw a recipe that she didn't want to try.

"Hey sweetie," she said as she greeted me with open arms for a hug. "I know you and Mia went out to eat, but I was hoping that you'd have some room to try at least one of these cookies. I've added an extra ingredient to the recipe and I want to see what you think."

Me turn down Mom's cookies? As if!

"Of course! Let me go get changed and I'll be right back."

"Great," mom said with a smile.

I raced upstairs and flung open the door to my room which reflected my artistic spirit. The walls were filled with my drawings, art prints from friends, and photographs of my family. I set down my backpack and hastily tidied up my room in order to find my comfy clothes. Note to self: do a deep cleaning of my room this summer.

Once I changed into my clothes, I walked down into the bathroom to wash my face from the day's grime. There was something that the simplicity of washing your face after a long day that was so relaxing. I looked in the mirror at my reflection: dark brown eyes, warm brown skin, and frizzy dark brown hair. The humidity was getting to my hair already and summer vacation had just started.

After washing and exfoliating my face, I walked back downstairs where I was greeted once again by the aroma of cookies. I sat down at the island in the kitchen where a plate of fresh cookies awaited me.

"They should be cool in a few minutes," said Mom, "but in the meantime, tell me all about your day. It's the last day of school so I'm sure lots of exciting things happened today."

I went over my school day and my meeting with Mia at Athens Coney Island. I told her about our big summer list and all of things that we were trying to accomplish this summer. My mom smiled and nodded enthusiastically. Though as I was looking at her face as I recapped the day's events I noticed something change in her facial expression and that usually meant something big was going to happen.

"What's with that look mom?" I stated. "Usually when you grin like that you have some pretty big news to share."

"I'll tell you in a minute," said mom, "but

first try these cookies."

I looked at her with slight suspicion, but reached for a cookie off the plate. As I bit into its gooey, chocolatey center, I noticed something different right off the bat. Was it cinnamon or brown sugar? I couldn't put my finger on it, but there was something about the flavor that had that extra kick to it.

"What's the special ingredient Mom? This is amazing!" I exclaimed.

My mom's eyes filled up with delight.

"I knew you would love it!" she replied. "But as I've said before. A cook never tells her secrets."

I rolled my eyes in fake annoyance.

"Okay, whatever you say Mom."

"Now for the big news," my mom said. "I know every summer I have you working on a project that involves some type of cleaning or restoration. We're still going to do that, however since it's the summer before you enter the 9th grade I wanted to do something special for you."

"Your dad and I know how much you love to draw, especially when it comes to animation, so we've been saving up to enroll you in a summer art program. It's being held at the local art college and its 6 weeks long. You'd get to work with some people in the industry and learn some new drawing techniques too!"

My jaw dropped. I was speechless. I had been not-so-subtly hinting to my parents that I wanted to participate in an art program for the longest time, but never in a million years did I actually think they would sign me up for one, let alone an animation art program!

I jumped up out of my chair and I gave my mom the biggest bear hug.

"Thank you so much," I said.

Words couldn't express how grateful I was, but my mom just knew by looking at me.

"I have always believed in your artwork, even though I don't say anything. You are so talented, sweetie. This will be a great opportunity for you, I know it!" said Mom.

Later that night, I lay in my bed smiling. Maybe this summer wouldn't be that bad after all.

♦

## CHAPTER TWO

I WOKE up as the sun's rays hit my face while lying in bed. It took me forever to get to sleep since I was so excited about the art class. I ended up sketching out various pieces at my art desk late into the night and even until the morning. When I finally did fall asleep, I didn't even remember what time it was. After yawning and stretching, I quickly hopped out of bed.

I walked over to the closet to see what I could wear to celebrate the first day of summer vacation. The class wouldn't start until later into the week so I still had time to start the deep cleaning of my room and whatever small project my mom would throw my way.

"What should I wear?" I questioned out loud to myself.

Settling on a romper and a t-shirt, I was

ready to start my day. I finished getting ready in the bathroom while humming a happy tune. I took a long shower to clear my head and got dressed.

When I was all finished, I walked down the stairs. It was quieter than usual, but I assumed both my parents were working and running errands. My dad worked the afternoon shifts at his job at General Motors so I didn't always get to see him in the evenings. I walked around to see if anyone was still home and glanced at the table in the dining room to see a note laying there. It read:

*Good Morning Nadia!*

*I tried to wake you, but you were sleeping so soundly I decided to let you sleep in. It is summer after all. If you look in the fridge, there's a breakfast casserole I left for you on the top shelf.*

*I know you want a lazy day at home, but if you could please tend to the garden and clean the living room it would be a big help. We'll talk about shopping for supplies for your art class after I get home from work.*

*Love you,*
*Mom*

"Ugh" I said out loud to myself as my echo rang through the empty house.

I rolled my eyes as I thought to myself, "not even one day of summer vacation passed and here I was already doing chores. Couldn't I have just have one day of relaxation?"

At least mom left some of her tasty casserole for me to eat. I put the note down on the table and walked over to the picture window in the living room. It seemed liked there were no clouds in the sky and that it was going to be a clear sunny day. The weather was on my side for once.

Stretching as I walked, I went over to the kitchen and opened the fridge to find the casserole sitting on the top shelf. I took the casserole out of the fridge and cut a generous slice for my breakfast. I went over to the cabinet, grabbed a plate on the shelf, and placed the casserole slice on the plate.

Though it was warm outside, I wanted a hot drink as well. Walking over to the sink I ran some water for the tea kettle that sat on the stove. My drink of choice was usually a frothy latte, but today I was feeling like having a hot cup of tea. As I microwaved the casserole and waited for my tea water to come to a boil, I pondered over my day.

I sat down with my food and ate quickly. The sooner I was done with my chores, the faster I could relax in my room. Since the sun was pretty high and it wasn't too hot yet, I thought I better start with the garden and then clean the living room. After washing my breakfast dishes, I gathered up the gardening supplies and headed outdoors. Walking over to the flower bushes I could smell the sweet aroma coming off the petals.

Like drawing, gardening was calming to me. The flowers were all in bloom and while I was watering them, I made a mental note to sketch a couple drawings before the summer heat made the flower petals wither.

Once I was finished cleaning up the garden, I headed indoors to clean up the living room. I took a double look at the clock and saw that it was already late in the afternoon. I guess I had spent more time outdoors than I thought!

I quickly put away the gardening supplies and grabbed the cleaning supplies for the living room. Mom would be home soon, so I had better hurry up since I know she liked to come home to a tidy house.

Once I was done with cleaning the living room, I was wiped out completely! I had ended up in one of my extreme cleaning modes and dusted the entire room from top to bottom. I heard my mom's car pull up in the driveway as I plopped down on the couch.

"Ughh," I thought. "So much for having some free time to myself today."

Maybe I should set up an alarm in the future? Although, the mere thought of waking up to an alarm during summer vacation left me groaning internally. I already woke up early enough as it was during the school year.

As the key entered the lock I heard my mom call out, "Nadia! I'm home," as she opened the door.

I walked over to the front door to greet my mom.

"Hey sweetie," she said, "How did it go today? I hope I didn't give you too much to do."

I could tell she felt a little guilty about asking me to clean up around the house on the first day of summer vacation. But I knew that she and my dad were always constantly working and didn't always have time to do household chores. Plus I wanted to stay in their good graces so I could still take the class.

"It went well. I got everything done, although we should probably stock up on cleaning supplies since we're a bit low," I replied.

"Thanks again!" she said, "Let me go get tidied up and we can make a trip to the craft store for your art class. I printed out your supply list at work so we can figure out what you need."

Within the next half hour we were out the door and on to our way to the Starry Night Craft Store. It was one of my favorite places to shop. It was a cute, little independent art shop that thrived on giving their customers the best personal shopping experience. The ceiling mirrored Van Gogh's *Starry Night* painting, and local artist's artwork lined the walls in an array of colors. The owner, Kim, was one of the sweetest people you could ever meet. She had a somewhat quirky vibe, but she knew her stuff when it came to art supplies and working with different mediums. One day I hoped I could work at a shop like hers, or even own my own art store in the future.

We pulled up to the downtown shopping area near our house in no time, quickly found a parking spot, and strolled down the block to the craft store. As I walked down the sidewalk I admired the sights and sounds of summer. People were out and about, enjoying the warm weather, shopping, and indulging in sweet treats such as ice cream. My mom and I eyed each other as we passed Mr. C's Sweets Shop and knew that we would be headed there right after picking up the art supplies.

After arriving at the store as we opened the door, we were immediately greeted by a "Hello," and then Kim came from around the corner of one of the aisles.

"Nadia! Mrs. Johnson! What a lovely surprise to see two of my favorite customers!" she said while smiling warmly. "How have you been," she asked as she enveloped us both in a hug.

"We've been good," we replied.

Kim asked what brought us in today as she straightened the glasses on her face.

"My little star artist is all grown up, so her father and I signed her up for summer art classes," my mom boasted loudly.

I tried not to groan out loud since the shop was not entirely empty, but my mom's voice had a tendency to carry across the room when she was excited. In other words, I felt just like a turtle that wanted to retreat into its shell. My mom and Kim started chattering amongst themselves while praising my skills.

I bent down to "tie" my shoe, but really it was a way for me to recover from embarrassment. Before I was finished fixing my shoes, I glanced up to see my mom showing Kim my supply list and they were off in a flash. Standing up I decided to catch up to them before they could go too far.

As I took a step forward, I felt like I was being watched. Slowly turning around, I locked eyes with a boy that looked to be about my age. He was looking back at me and was pretty cute too. I quickly turned away, but not without him seeing him smile back at me. Too embarrassed to speak, I quickly jogged off towards the direction in which I could hear my mom and Kim chattering away.

When I met up with them, my eyes widened with surprise to see the both of their hands filled with art supplies. They felt my presence as I arrived in the aisle and their conversation bubble quickly burst as they came back to reality. They looked at me sheepishly and then down at the large array of art supplies they held in their hands.

"I guess we both got a bit carried away," said my mom. "Let's go over to the checkout area and we can sift through some of these supplies to see what best might be suited for you" said Kim.

I took some of the art supplies out of their hands to help carry them to the register while they juggled the rest of the supplies in their arms. After organizing all the items on the counter, Kim handed me the class syllabus' supply sheet and I glanced over the items on the list:

- Comic Strip Boards
- Sketchbook
- Fine Tip Pens & Markers
- Sketching Pencils

Sounded simple enough to me, I said as I looked over the class syllabus sheet. I questioned Kim about the supplies that she recommended to me and which ones worked the best. She was a bit familiar with the materials I liked to use and had seen some of my cartooning pieces. Once I selected the best products for me, Kim rung up my items at the register and my mom and I said our goodbyes. As we left the store we made a beeline for Mr. C's for some ice cream.

"Dad will be home for dinner tonight. Since it's finally summer, I say we pick up some pizza for dinner to celebrate the season," mom said.

"When have I ever turned down pizza?" I asked rhetorically.

My favorite food was pizza, so I wasn't complaining. We hopped back into the car after enjoying our ice cream sundaes, picked up a pizza, and headed home.

Later that night at dinner, my parents and I ate together. Both of them told me how proud of me they were. I couldn't wait for this summer to get started.

◆

## CHAPTER THREE

WAKING UP to my alarm, I excitedly jumped out of bed to turn it off. Today was the big day! My art class was finally beginning.

I did a little shimmy celebration dance in my pajamas when I heard my phone ping. Looking down at my phone, I saw a text from Mia wishing me good luck for the first day of classes along with a selfie of her giving me a thumbs up from the beach. She had a goofy grin on grin on her face as she posed next to the water with a summer dress and signature curly hair.

"Thanks girl," I wrote back to her, "bring back some of that Florida sun and sand on your way home!"

Putting my phone down, I walked over to my closet to decide what to wear. Maybe I was making too much of a big deal of it but I wanted to make a good first impression.

Putting together an outfit that I considered artist hipster chic, my final selection consisted of a *Sailor Moon* t-shirt, ripped skinny jeans, and a beret to top it all off. I raced to the bathroom to get cleaned up as I heard my mom call out my name.

"Nadia," she shouted from downstairs.

"Yes?" I replied loudly.

"Breakfast is ready! Hurry up so we won't be late dropping you off. I'd like to get there a bit early," she said.

"No problem!" I said.

I sprinted to the bathroom. So maybe I had spent a bit too much time picking out an outfit, but it was essential to look my best.

After getting ready, I raced down the stairs to the kitchen. Glancing at the clock on the wall, my eyes widened in surprise when I saw what time it was.

"9:30?" I exclaimed out loud as my Mom walked into the kitchen.

"I was hoping you'd be ready sooner, but it looks like you'll have to eat breakfast on-the-go now," my mom replied.

I groaned outwardly. This day was not getting off to a great start at all.

Fast forward to the car; Mom drove while I sat in the passenger seat attempting to scarf my breakfast down as quickly as I could. Riding over the bumps in the road made everything twice as difficult and I struggled to balance the container that held my oatmeal. All of a sudden, mom slammed on the brakes as the car in front of us came to a hard stop.

It was like something out a sitcom, as I watched in super slow-motion, horrified as the oatmeal flew out of the container and into my lap. Mom asked if I was okay, but she then saw the food on my lap and immediately grabbed some Kleenex from the backseat.

"Sorry sweetie," she said with a regretful face.

"It's fine" I replied, but on the inside I felt like withering away. In my mind I shouted, "Please let nothing else go wrong with this day!"

I cleaned the mess off my jeans as best as I could. Hopefully they wouldn't get stained.

We finally arrived at the community center, where I was being dropped off.

"You'll do great Nadia. Have a good day," she said.

"I will. Have fun at work Mom," I tried to put a grin on my face.

After waking up late and spilling breakfast all over my pants, my morale was a bit low. I was excited this morning, but as I grabbed my supplies and headed towards the sidewalk in front of the building, I started to feel a bit anxious.

So many questions crossed my mind. What kind of people would be in this class? Were my drawings mediocre? Do I even have the skills to learn cartooning? I did the best to shake the negative thoughts from my mind and stay positive. I was able to clean most of my spilled breakfast on my pants so at least I wouldn't be nicknamed as "oat girl."

Stepping into the classroom, I looked around for an empty seat and hastily made my way towards it. Sitting all the way in the back wasn't my first choice, but it didn't help that I didn't get here early.

As a looked around the room, there were people my age and older chatting about everything and anything. It was nice to see such a diverse classroom of people. I felt a friendly vibe from the other students and I was hoping to make more art friends.

After setting my stuff down on the table, I turned around to greet my seat buddy. As my eyes landed on him, I realized it was the boy from the Starry Night Craft Store.

Looking up close I could see him more in detail. Broad nose, tan skin, freckles, and a nice set of dimples.

"Quick! Nadia say something so you don't seem like a creep," I said in my mind. "Hello, my name is Nadia," I said to him

"Nice to meet you." He greeted me and spoke with a warm smile that I remembered from yesterday. "Hey, my name's Aiden. Nice to meet you too," he replied. "You're the girl from the art store yesterday, right?" he asked.

"Yep, that's me. Do you go to Starry Night often?" I asked.

"Actually it was only my second time shopping there, but it's good to see a familiar face," he said.

I blushed hard and before I could reply, the

teacher stepped into the room.

"Hello everyone! It's nice to see you all. My name is Benjamin Rider, but you all can call me Ben or Mr.Rider."

"I hope that you've all come to this class to hone your artistic skills, learn something new, as well as learn from each other. This isn't school, so I don't expect this class to be too demanding for you all, but I do want you all to take away something from this summer course and most of all have fun!" said Mr. Rider.

Right off the bat he gave a good impression and had a warm friendly vibe that everyone seemed to respond to. I could tell everyone else was a bit anxious too.

"A little about me," said Mr. Rider as he continued. "I've had a passion for art since I was a kid and there was always something about the world of cartoons and animation that followed me. I took various art classes during my school years, but it wasn't until I was in college that I became serious about my studies. It was at Northwestern University that I started to hone my skills."

"From there I was able to go on into the

industry where I started out as an intern at Art
Boss Studios where I worked on storyboards for
a few small animation shorts. From there I went
on to Plexus where I spent several years working
my way up to be the head animator until I left
to start teaching. Then I ended up here with you
all," he said with a smile on his face.

I was thoroughly impressed. Even though
I was expecting a regular art teacher like other
art classes I had in school, this guy was a pro.
Art Boss may not be the biggest studio, but to
land an internship like that was a big deal. They
fostered some of the greatest cartoonists and
animators that became well known. I looked
around and saw that everyone else was in awe
too. Even if you weren't an artist, those names
were still familiar to many people.

"I won't ramble on too much longer so that
we can get started," he continued. "But I really
look forward to getting to know each and every
one of you. Though the class is advertised as
cartooning, I thought it would mix that and
animation into our course."

"Now let's go through some introductions.
Starting counter clockwise I want you to go

around the room and introduced yourselves." he stated.

It looked like I would be last, which I wasn't too happy about. Each person went around the room sharing their name, favorite cartoon, and why they loved the cartoon and animation medium.

Once it got to Aiden, he stood up and said, "Hi! My name's Aiden. My favorite cartoon is *Castle in the Sky* by Studio Ghibli and I love cartoons because they hold so much nostalgia for people of all ages."

"A Studio Ghibli fan," I pondered, "it looks like we have something in common after all," I thought with a smile on my face.

Aiden sat down and then it was my turn. I looked at the room as everyone waited for me to speak.

Standing up I said, "Hey, my name's Nadia. My favorite cartoon is *Sailor Moon*, as it's pretty evident by my t-shirt I'm wearing." A few people chuckled. "I love cartoons because they push the boundaries of the imagination. With a cartoon you can bring any idea to life and I think there's something amazing about that."

As I sat down in my seat, I could see Mr. Rider and other classmates nod in agreement.

I looked over my left shoulder to see Aiden giving me a thumbs up.

"Japanese animation is pretty cool," he stated.

I smiled in reply and before I could respond, Mr. Rider launched into his lecture of the history of animation and what we would expect during this summer course. Throughout the whole class I felt as if Aiden and I kept sneaking glances at one other. There was something there for sure.

◆

# Lost Love: My First Boyfriend

## CHAPTER FOUR

THE CLASS lasted most of the day since it was an extended summer course (scheduled two days a week.) By the end of the first day of class, I felt rejuvenated and excited to learn more. It was almost 3pm when we finished for the day and I pulled my phone out of my bag to see if my mom was here to pick me. I looked down to see a text saying "waiting in front" from Mom and carefully packed the rest of the items in my bag.

Aiden said, "see you later desk mate," and walked out of the classroom as I waved goodbye.

Making sure I didn't leave everything behind I put my bag on my shoulder and walked outside to the car.

Memories of the day ran through my mind and it made me smile. During our lunch break,

Aiden and I sat down with the rest of our classmates to get to know each other. After getting to know one another, it felt as if we had known each other for a long time. Aiden was an artist like me and loved to focus on still life drawing, but also dabbled in drawing cartoons.

He had moved to Michigan a couple of years ago from San Francisco with his family and went to a nearby school in the area. He told me about some of his artistic adventures while growing up and some of the art museums he had visited.

I smiled all the way on the car ride home, and I noticed that my mom kept sneaking glances at me as she drove.

"What's that big smile on your face for?" she asked.

"It's nothing," "I replied, "I just had a very good day."

"Seems like you met a cute boy to me," she replied. "My mom senses are tingling. So something good must have happened."

I tried so hard to hide myself blushing. My mom always seemed to be an expert at reading expressions, especially mine. I found it really hard to show what I was feeling on my face.

Trying to play it off, I said, "Nah it's nothing like that. I just feel really good about this class. I met some awesome people that have a lot of common interests. I just know that I'm going to learn a lot from this class. And hopefully this will help me when I go off to high school and college."

"I'm just teasing you Nadia," my mom said laughing, "I know you are excited about this class. I think this will provide a lot of opportunities for you."

I smiled hearing my Mom's words and it made me feel good that she was proud of me. I know that some parents weren't always accepting of their kids wanting a career in the arts, but I was thankful she was open-minded about it. I still knew though that deep down inside that I needed to show her and dad how serious I was about this.

After dinner that night, I went up to my room and ate while brainstorming ideas for my own personal project that I had been working on. It was a spoof story about a female superhero that had quirky superpowers. I hadn't worked on it much lately since I was busy at school and wanted to finish some of the concept art so that I could show it to Mr. Rider at some time in the summer and hopefully get some feedback.

Since the class started on Thursday and we only met on Tuesdays and Thursdays, I had some time over the weekend to work on the first assignment for our class. Mr. Rider wanted us to share a bit of animation history and our task was to write about and share our favorite cartoon and give the history of it.

Like I stated in class earlier that day, my project would be on *Sailor Moon*. Though it was considered a retro cartoon, you couldn't deny its influence on the animation world. It was a "magical girl" themed story with girl power vibes and it really resonated with me as a young child. Serena was fierce, kind, and knew how to save the day. I even based my female superhero story off of the comic.

I made a mental note to start on my project during the weekend, now it was time to sketch. Grabbing my phone and plugging in my headphones, I set the music to one of my favorite playlists and got to work.

◊　◊　◊

Feeling the sun on my face through the window, I opened my bleary eyes to a new day. As usual I had spent most of the night at my desk sketching away. Before I knew it, time got away from me and I ended up going to bed around 1:00 AM. I yawned and then slowly rose out of bed.

I didn't hear any moving around downstairs so I guess my parents had already left for work. As I opened the window, I heard a faint singing that could only be my dad's voice. He must be working from home or had the day off. Quickly looking around my room left me a bit horrified at how cluttered it was. I'd been so busy with school and helping out with chores that I hadn't cleaned my room.

I walked back over to my nightstand, glanced at my phone and saw no new messages. Whew!

Maybe there were no chores today. Although with dad being at home I figured he probably needed help with some kind of project. Turning my music up on my mp3 app, I went around tidying my room so I could at least find things again. After I was finished, I decided to take a morning shower to get my day jumpstarted. I got dressed and went downstairs to find my dad relaxing on the couch.

"Morning honey!" he said.

"Hey, dad?" I said as I sat on the couch next to him, "No work today?"

"Nah," he replied. "I felt like playing hooky."

I laughed while giving him a skeptical look in my eyes. "Doesn't seem very responsible to me," I said.

"Sometimes we need a little relaxing now and then," he said, "But in all honestly I took the day off to get some projects done."

"Want to help out?" he asked, "We can count them as part of your chores list. Your mom left a list of stuff for you to do."

On the one hand, helping out dad wouldn't hurt; on the other hand I wasn't keen on spending each of my summer days cooped up inside. I pondered my options briefly and then I made my decision.

"I can help out," I replied, "What's on the agenda for today?"

"Well now that I've finished all of the gardening stuff, there are still some more tasks to do out in the backyard. I was going focus on the shed today. So let's hop on over to the hardware store." he said.

Soon we had the car all prepped in the backseat and off we went to the hardware store. My dad and I sang along to old songs on the radio as we rode in the car. I loved that my dad had such a carefree spirit. He always knew how to make anyone laugh when they were having a bad day.

Pulling into the hardware store's parking lot, I got really excited. This was one of my favorite places to go, and it reminded me a larger version of the craft store. Even though my dad was a handyman, I liked to think of his hardware projects as art. Maybe that's where I got some of my creativity from. I followed him through the aisle until we landed in the paint section.

My dad stopped and turned out around to say, "Today's project is painting the shed!"

I wasn't the best painter, since drawing was more of my thing, but how hard could it be?

"We'll each pick out some colors and then decide what's best," he said.

We split up and I hunted for the best colors that would suit the shed, but at the same time compliment the garden. After spending some time debating over colors, we came to a decision. We bought the rest of the painting supplies, but not before the nearby hot dog stand caught our eyes. Even as a kid I always thought that having a hot dog stand in a hardware store was weird. But once you feasted on the hot dogs, your worries were washed away. We headed to the car to drop off the supplies, and then made our way back to the hot dog stand for a summertime treat.

Once at home, we got all dressed up in painting gear, and then set off to work.

"I thought this time would be a good time for us to catch up since I've been working so much overtime lately," my dad said. "What's been going on lately? How is your art class working for you?"

"It's been good so far. I do miss hanging out with Mia. So I'm kind of bummed about not being able to share part of the summer with my best friend," I replied. "I'm still trying to get used to summer."

"Don't worry about it," he said while

painting the shed, "She'll be home before you know it. Why don't you trying setting up a Skype chat with her this weekend? I'm sure she'd have some downtime to talk with you," he said.

I hadn't thought about that. Maybe I should reach out to her later on and see if she could chat. I know she was busy with her family vacation so I didn't want to take too much of her time. I made a mental note to text her later on.

"How's your art class going?" he asked.

"Well it's very interesting so far. There are a lot of fun people in my class and the teacher, Mr. Rider is awesome." I explained as my eyes lit up with joy, "he's done so much work in the animation field and he's got a warm personality."

My dad nodded to show that he was listening as he started touching up some of the small crevices on the shed with paint in concentration.

"I know I've only had one class so far, but I feel a little anxious deep down inside to be honest. This is such a big deal for me. I've never really had my art critiqued at all and I'm worried that my drawings aren't that good," I said.

My dad put his paintbrush down inside the

paint bucket and took a deep look at me.

"I know that trying new things can be scary, but if you don't ever jump out of your comfort zone how will you know?" he said. "You are incredibly talented Nadia, so don't ever doubt yourself. If there's something that you have difficulty with, you have to keep trying at it until you improve. You got this, sweetie," he said while giving me a hug.

I was touched by his words and it was the motivating factor that I needed to hear at that moment. Instead of goofing off like I used to do each summer, I needed to use this free time that I had to focus on my art more. Sure, I could balance fun with work, but I need to be more serious about my time management. There was no way I was going to get out of chores during the summer, but the least I could do was spend more time practicing drawing.

"Thanks dad, that's what I needed to hear," I said.

"It's the powers that be when you're a wise dad like me," he joked.

We both laughed and continued to work into the shed painting project until late in the

44

day.

Later that evening, I messaged Mia to see if she could Skype soon. We had a lot to catch up on since we hadn't really talked after she left for Florida for vacation. Immediately I heard a ping notification on my phone to see that she texted back.

She wrote, "Yes! My family is driving me crazy at the moment. Plus we need to catch up on some girl talk. Is now a good time?" she asked.

I wrote, "Sure, let me sign into Skype."

Booting up the site, I signed in and video called Mia.

"Hey girl!" she said as her face popped up on the screen. "Long time no talk."

"I miss you so much! How's Florida?" I asked.

"It's been pretty good so far, besides my family driving me crazy. The weather is so gorgeous here Nadia. I wish you could have come with us!" she replied. "It's been really nice to spend some more time with my grandparents though. I haven't seen them in a while so it's been nice to be able to catch up with them," she said.

"How's the art class so far? Are you the next Frida Kahlo or the next Van Gogh?" she asked with dramatic flair.

"Ha ha," I laughed in response. "Not hardly, but we've only had one class so far. But who knows what will happen next?"

"I'm so proud of you though, I wish I could draw like you." she said.

"I do want to tell you one thing though," I continued, "I met a boy in my class."

Mia squealed with joy and clapped her hands. "Tell me all about him!" she said.

And so I launched into the story of how I met Aiden, and we gossiped about boys all night.

♦

## CHAPTER FIVE

BEFORE I knew it, the weekend had passed and it was time to go to class again. I finished my homework project with ease and I was excited to get back to class. I was looking forward to talking to Aiden again and my face was flushed just thinking about him. He was smart, kind, adventurous, and I liked that we had many things in common and hit it off so well.

There was a spark between the two of us that I felt deeply. I had never met someone like him before. I didn't want to get too ahead of myself and get all giddy. I wanted to stay grounded and be realistic, maybe we could be something more, or maybe we would be just friends. And if it was the latter, I had to be okay with it since I didn't want to lose his companionship.

Walking into the classroom I saw the room half full. Mr. Rider wasn't there yet and people were still starting to trickle in. Thankfully I had gotten up even earlier this morning so I wouldn't be the last person to arrive. Walking to my seat I was greeted by Linda, a thirty-some-thing mom of two who had a very eccentric spirit. Linda ran her own online art shop in her free time, but her main job was as an accoun-tant since she was a single mom supporting her two kids. She had a warm, inviting spirit and after seeing some of her sketches from the week before, I knew I could learn a lot from her.

"Hey girlie!" Linda exclaimed, "How was your weekend?"

"It was pretty good Linda," I replied. "How was yours?"

"Now that the kids are on summer break, they've been helping around the house more. It's great since I got to work on a couple of pieces that I've have been wanting to finish. Let me ask your opinion on these pieces," said Linda as she pulled out her tablet.

Whereas Linda focused on digital art, I was used to drawing in more of the traditional style.

Hopefully, I could get a summer job in the next couple of years so that I could save up to buy a drawing tablet. Though the basic ones came pretty cheap, I still needed to save for a better computer to be able to work on digital content.

I sifted through the pieces she showed me and helped her pick out a few that she should add to her shop.

"Thanks Nadia!" she said, "I really appreciate it."

It was still hard to me to get used to giving feedback or suggestions on other people's art, but I was starting to become more comfortable with it. Like it or not, if I actually decided that if I was going to continue in the animation industry in the future, that was just a part of the job that I was going to have to get used to.

Walking over to my seat I set my art bag on the floor next to me. Since it was a community center, the classrooms were a lot smaller and the desk space was narrow enough as it was. Pulling my sketchbook out of my bag, I decided to work on some of my comic sketches before Aiden arrived.

Caught up in my drawings, I was so focused

on sketching that I didn't even hear Aiden sit down next to me. It wasn't until that I felt a soft tap on my left shoulder that I looked up to see him smiling at me.

"Morning Nadia, what's up? I hope I didn't scare you." Aiden said grinning.

"Hi! Sorry about that! Sometimes when I'm drawing I get so focused and lost in my thoughts," I replied.

"It's no problem," he laughed, "And if you don't mind me asking, what are you working on?" he asked.

I told him a bit about my comic book project I had started and he nodded while listening to me.

"That's pretty cool," he said. "I've always wanted to come up with my own project, but found it a bit daunting. My schedule is pretty hectic during the school year, so I don't get much time as I'd like to draw as much as I want to."

I grinned at hearing his words of admiration as I thought to myself, "Girl you have got to get a hold of yourself."

Before we could continue our conversation,

Mr. Rider cleared his throat and the conversations in the classroom came to an absolute halt.

"So to start off with today's lesson, we'll go around the room and present our projects that I assigned from last week," he stated. "You aren't necessarily being graded on your presentation, but I do expect to show that you put in effort in your artwork and what research you came up with," he continued. "Just do your best and have fun with it! We're all friends here!"

One by one, each person came up to share their favorite cartoons and I found that some of their personal favorites were mine too. There were presentations that ranged from classic cartoons created during the early age of animation, to even more recent ones. I was amazed by all of the artwork as well. Each person added their own touch to make their project more personal.

When my time came to present, I found myself feeling less anxious than I was when I had woken up that morning. Aiden gave me a quick thumbs up from our table, and I launched into my presentation. I had a lot of fun sharing my stories of nostalgia about *Sailor Moon* like others did with their presentations. Instead of talking to a room full of strangers, I felt like I was talking to a room full of friends.

As I ended my presentation, I felt satisfied with myself for conquering some of my public-speaking fears. A few more presentations came after mine, and then we were back to class mode.

Mr. Rider got up to speak in front of the classroom, "Like with our first lesson, we'll be continuing our focus on the founding principles of animation today, and then on Thursday we'll be focusing on the basic concepts of physics and how they apply to animated motion, emotion, and acting.," he stated. "Now where were we?" he asked to himself out loud as he flipped to his notes.

I got out my sketchbook to take down some notes from the class. I was familiar with many basics of animation, but it couldn't hurt for me to refresh my memory on some aspects.

At noon it was time for lunch and since it was such a nice day outside, everyone headed outdoors to eat on the patio and lawn again. I could smell the lovely aroma of the flowers outside of the community center as I walked outside with the rest of the class. It was so nice to be outside. The breeze was warm and it wasn't too hot either. Sitting down at one of the patio tables, I started to unpack my lunch when I heard a voice beside me.

"Is this seat taken?" he said.

And I looked up to see Aiden sitting down next to me. I smiled in response. We had been so busy for the first part of the class that we hadn't gotten much time to continue our conversation from this morning.

"Nice presentation," I said.

I was thoroughly impressed with the amount of research that he did and his sketches. Aiden focused on classic *Looney Tunes* cartoons for his presentation and drew pictures of its iconic characters in different tourist spots of the city.

"Thanks," he replied. "Yours was good too, I really liked your sketches."

"Thanks," I replied.

I wasn't sure what to say to him. We hadn't really talked too much outside of class and we were usually sitting with the rest of our class-mates. It was just a little bit a bit awkward and

I could feel that we were both trying to think of words to help fill some of the silence. We would slightly glance up at each other from our lunches to acknowledge each other and then would go back to eating again.

"Come on Nadia," I thought to myself, "think of something creative or witty to say to him, and quick."

Mulling over conversation topics in my head, I remembered my goals that I wanted to achieve at the beginning of the summer. I wanted to push myself more outside the box and be more confident. Finally a conversation topic popped up in my head!

"Aiden," I turned around to speak.

"Hmm?" he said, looking up from his lunch.

"You said you moved a lot with your family; what made you guys move here?" I asked.

"Well," he replied, "My dad travels a lot for his job as a tech consultant and we've had to relocate a few times because of it. I think we moved here not only for my dad's job, but also for a change of pace. Everyplace we've been except here has been a fast-paced kind of life-style. And that's not to say that this part of the

Midwest isn't bustling because we still live in the city, but it's different."

I could understand that. Even though were a busy metropolitan area, we were still were far removed from a lot of the bigger cities like New York.

"If you don't mind me asking, what are some of the favorite places you lived in?"

I could see him mull the question over in his mind as his eyebrows furrowed in concentration.

"Well, I enjoyed New Orleans because of its rich culture, Memphis for all of the sights and sounds, and San Francisco because of its artsy vibes," said.

I didn't realize he had traveled that much. The most travelling I had done was going to Florida a couple of times, but mostly I just traveled within my home state of Michigan. I loved going to state parks in the summertime and sometimes my family and I would go to places like Mackinac Island. I still considered myself to be lucky to even be able to travel anywhere.

"That's so cool that you've had the opportunity to travel to so many places," I said.

"Yeah, it is," Aiden said. "it has been amazing to live in some the places I have, and I don't want to sound ungrateful, but it was hard as a kid moving around from place to place. My little brother Jake and I always had to change schools and it was hard to maintain friendships because once we got settled, it was hard to get adjusted to a place all over again."

Before I started to feel green-eyed about my own life's experiences, I thought about what he said and how lonely it must have been for him when he was younger.

"That sounds like it must have been difficult for you," I said.

"It's a bit easier now that I'm older, but when I was little it was very hard on me, and especially so for my parents for having to constantly adjust to new places. We've been here for a while, but I've always had some fear in the back of my mind that we'll have to end up moving again because of my dad's job. It's not like I have much of a choice, but I'd like to stay in one spot before I go to college," he said.

I could tell the subject of moving brought him down a bit so I decided to change the subject. Luckily, the moment I thought of that one of my classmates, Yoona, came over to invite us to play Pictionary.

"Come on Aiden, let's play." I said.

"Sure" he said with a smile.

As we packed up our lunches to go sit with the others where the game was set up, I felt Aiden tug on my shoulder. I turned to look at him.

"By the way, I wanted to ask you if you wanted to go to this art exhibition at Belle Isle Park this weekend?" he asked.

I could tell he was trying not to get flustered, but I could see his face get red. Was this a date?, I thought to myself. I could feel a smile forming on my face and I tried to keep my emotions in check.

"It's not like a date, by my mom was going to go anyway I thought it would be something you'd be interested in," he continued.

"Not a date," I thought. I won't lie that my happy little bubble burst.

"Sure," I answered, "Let me get your number and you can text me all the details."

I was a bit disappointed but was going to

keep my hopes up. Maybe this *was* a date and he was just trying to keep things casual. Or maybe he just wanted to be friends. Only time would tell.

♦

## CHAPTER SIX

BEFORE I knew, it the weekend was here! Finally, a little time for some relaxation and my big date, or "non-date" according to Aiden's description. It was time for the big day and I couldn't wait to go to Belle Isle. It was such a beautiful park that was surrounded by the river and it housed an aquarium, conservatory, nature center, and more. I looked forward to going to the outdoor exhibition since I had missed out on a lot of the art shows last year.

I had sat down with my mom earlier in the week, and she found out about Aiden before I could tell about her myself. I could hardly sit down on the living room couch for movie night that evening before she exclaimed, "You met a boy! I knew it."

My mouth dropped open in surprise. How

could moms guess everything? It was like they had superpowers or something.

I had told her about Aiden, where he was from, and about his artwork. My mom told me based on my description alone that she had gotten a good vibe from him.

Then I told her about our "non-date" and she just rolled her eyes at me and said, "This is obviously a date. He just wants to make you feel more comfortable by not putting pressure on you."

I honestly hadn't thought about it, but I guess it was a *kind of* date. I didn't think his mom would be hanging out with us the entire time since he explained that some of her friends would be participating in the exhibition.

Changing my mind to think of this as a date, I agonized about what to wear to the park. Should I be casual or more dressed up? I pulled up the weather app on my phone and saw that it would be a blazing hot day. Maybe I should go with a casual yet dressy combo.

Rifling through my closet I picked out a couple of options of what to wear. I ended up putting on a t-shirt dress and paired it with my

*Converse* shoes. I knew I would be doing a lot of walking around so I wanted to be comfortable. After I finished getting ready, I went downstairs and looked for my backpack to take with me.

My mom said from the kitchen, "If you're looking for your backpack, it's in here."

Man, she was scary good about that kind of stuff. Sometimes I felt like she had a sixth sense when it came to most stuff.

"Hurry up," she said, "so we can get on the road. I need to run some errands, plus I don't want you to be late for you big day."

Driving in the car, I tried not to make myself anxious. I rolled the window down and felt the breeze in my face. Twenty minutes later, we were at the park and parked near the James Scott Fountain where Aiden said we would meet up.

My mom and I got out of the car and started walking towards the fountain where I soon saw Aiden and his mom waving us over to them. My mom and Aiden's mom exchanged greetings. Then my mom introduced herself to Aiden. My mom said her goodbyes and gave me a subtle wink before walking off and heading back to the car.

Aiden's mom then spoke up and said, "Nadia, it's great that you could come to this art exhibition today. I'll be a bit preoccupied with helping my friends out at their booths. You kids have fun and enjoy the show. I'll meet up with you a bit later."

We waved goodbye as she walked off towards the artist alley and we were left alone.

There was a moment of awkward silence between the two of us and then Aiden spoke.

"You look really nice today Nadia."

"Thanks," I replied feeling my face heat up.

Seeing that he had a pair of Converse sneakers on as well, I pointed down at his shoes and said, "hey we're matching today!"

He looked down and laughed and said "It seems so."

We then launched into a small conversation about sneakers while trying to break the ice between us. Was this a sign from the universe tell me that we would end up together? We were still getting to know one other, plus we hadn't really talked much outside of class.

Aiden pulled out a map of the art show and we took a look around at what they had to offer. Since we wanted to make sure that we saw as much stuff as possible, we decided to walk around the art fair counter-clockwise while stopping at a few of the park's attractions if we had the time.

Though it was starting to heat up outside, thankfully the clouds were providing some shade for the moment. The cool breeze off of the river was a welcome reprieve for us and many of the other park goers. While we spent some time in silence walking around, it was nice just to be able to spend some time together.

We started to talk about the different art pieces we liked and learned more about what types of art we enjoyed outside of animation. We spoke to various artists at the booths and got to learn more about their backstories and how they got started with their artwork. Once we mentioned that we were in a cartooning class, many of the artist's interests became piqued.

They were so kind and welcoming to us, all the while offering words of encouragement about our field of study. So many of the artists offered great advice about developing our art style.

One artist stated "It's important to not follow the crowd when it comes to your art journeys. Make sure to stay true to yourself and focus on creating your own art. It won't be easy, but it will help you in the long run."

After we decided to take a lunch break, Aiden and I bought some Detroit-style pizza which was my favorite. It's more of a rectangular pizza than a round pizza that has a thick crisp crust and toppings. He ordered a Hawaiian style pizza while I stuck with my regular order of pepperoni. Finding an empty picnic table to enjoy our lunch, we sat down and started to eat.

"How are you enjoying the exhibition so far?" Aiden asked.

"I really like it. Thanks for bringing me here. I haven't been to this exhibition before so it's all new to me," I replied.

"I'm glad you like it," Aiden said with a deep smile showing off his dimples. "Honestly, I was a bit worried about bringing you here. I wanted a chance to get to know you better outside of class. I think you're really cool and I like hanging out with you," he said.

My eyes lit up with happiness.

"I like spending time with you too," I said smiling.

I knew what we both felt at that moment, but couldn't find the courage to speak the words out loud to each other. We both got silent for a while and continued to eat our pizza.

I was trying to keep it cool on the outside, but on the inside I was an absolute mess. My inner self was dancing with joy. Maybe this was a date after all.

After lunch, we went to a couple of more booths and I asked Aiden if he had ever been to the nature conservatory on the island. He said he hadn't, so I decided to show him around the place.

The Anna Scripps Whitcomb Conservatory has an amazing collection of plants from around the world. Going around the conservatory, we looked around at all of the various plants and flowers. My grandmother instilled in me my love of gardening from a very young age so this place meant a lot to me. As we walked around, I pointed out some of my favorite plants and shared some information about them.

I could tell that he was thoroughly impressed

by my knowledge of plants and it was cool to see that someone wasn't weirded out by the fact that I was a walking garden encyclopedia. The conservatory was a bit humid so it wasn't crowded, but it was a nice time for us to talk more about things we enjoyed outside of art.

I felt really comfortable around him and some of the awkwardness that we had from earlier started to fade away. It was nice to be in each other's company and learn more about each other.

Once we finished going through the conservatory, we decided to take one more detour before heading back to the art show. We grabbed some ice cream from one of the many food trucks that lined the street and headed towards the benches by the water to sit and people watch.

Looking around, there were so many people fishing, feeding the ducks, and sitting by the water and basking in the sun. The sights and sounds of summer were always comforting to me. We continued to chat while enjoying the scenery around us. This was one of the times that I wish I had my sketchbook with me, but

I'd left it at home since I didn't want to carry it around all day. There were so many pictures I could sketch at that moment!

"I wish I had brought my sketchbook with me," Aiden said.

"You too?" I replied, "I was just thinking the same thing."

It was as if we both read each other's minds. We both shrugged our shoulders and tried to enjoy the rest of our time together even though we both wished we had some paper and pencil to draw with.

After some time, we met back up with Aiden's mom and met the rest of her art friends who were kind enough to let us take one of their smaller pieces home with them. It was getting late in the day and soon it was time to go back home. Back at the fountain, I waited for my mom to pick me up and I chatted with Aiden and his mom about our day. Before I knew it, my mom had arrived and it was time to go home.

Getting into the car, I greeted my mom and we drove off while waving goodbye. I spilled all of the details to my mom about my day and kept a permanent smile on my face.

Aiden was sweet, kind, and thoughtful. I had never had a guy ask me to go to an art exhibition before so it was a brand-new experience for me. Though I was nervous for most of the day, I found him really easy to talk to. It was comfortable, kind of like when I hung with friends or family, but I could tell that something was definitely blooming between us.

I spent the rest of the weekend walking around in a daze. I kept replaying our Belle Isle "non-date" over and over in my mind. Every time I thought about it, my stomach became full of butterflies.

On Sunday, I hopped on a quick *Skype* chat with Mia and told her everything in detail. She oohed and aahed during the entire play-by-play of our day of our "non-date."

"Where is my dream boyfriend to take me away from my crazy family and whisk me off into the sunset?" she said while sighing dramatically.

I couldn't help but laugh.

I told Mia, "Who knows, maybe a secret merman is waiting to confess his undying love for you on the beach."

"You're so silly, you know that?" she replied, "That's why you are my best friend."

"What's going to happen next? Will you guys go out again? Are you dating? Does he *like you* like you?" she asked in rapid fire succession.

"Slow down Mia! I have no idea, I mean, we just met and I'm not sure what this is," I said.

We had just met only a couple of weeks ago so I felt that things were very new between us.

"Well," Mia said, "Not to worry you but before you know it, June will be over. You and I know just how fast summer vacation can go by, and I just think at some point soon, you both should know where you stand on things."

I kept mulling over her words, thinking she was right when I sat down to think about it. Summer vacation went by fast. Though I had the rest of summer to figure things out, I knew the closer it got to starting school, that the harder it would be to spend some time together.

"Most importantly," she said, "I just don't want you to get hurt. You're like a sister to me and I know how compassionate you are."

"Don't rush into anything though. Just think

it over," she said.

Her words weighed heavily on my mind even after our *Skype* chat ended. I laid on my bed thinking. I was grateful for Mia's love guru advice, but at the same time I was a bit anxious. Was this just a summer fling? Or would it lead to be something more?

◆

## CHAPTER SEVEN

WHILE HEADING back to the art class on Tuesday, so many thoughts crossed my mind. When I walked into the classroom, it felt like I was in a daze. Sitting down in my seat, I looked up to see that I had arrived early and that most of the seats around me were empty.

Linda waved hi to me from her seat and came over to chat with me about her weekend. I drew in my sketchbook while she told me about this new virtual art museum website that had launched over the weekend. Nodding my head to show that I was listening while she talked I couldn't help but feel my mind wander.

Noticing I that I seemed far away, Linda looked at me and asked "what's wrong Nadia, I haven't seen you look so troubled."

I paused before replying, I didn't want to sound trivial by saying I had boy problems. I didn't really know how to talk about this stuff.

I shrugged my shoulders and replied, "It's nothing, I guess it's just my anxiety getting the best of me."

She looked at me deeply and said, "Well, if you ever want to talk, I'm here to listen no matter what. I'm a mom so I know when something is wrong."

"What is it with moms and their sixth sense?" I asked bewildered.

"It's a mom thing," she replied. "You'll understand when you get older."

Seeing that I could use some space she walked back over to her seat. Maybe I was overthinking things too much again. Like Mia said, I should just take things one day at a time.

I was also nervous since today was the day I finally built up the courage to ask Mr. Rider to see my artwork and give me some constructive feedback. I wasn't used to showing many people my artwork, but I knew in order to learn how to improve my drawing techniques, I needed critiquing. Everyone in the class as well as my closest friends told me I should do it and assured me that Mr. Rider was very approachable and easy to talk to. I had no doubts about that, but I was still overcome with anxiety.

I drew my hair up into a top knot since the weather was humid and my hair kept falling into my face. Fanning myself, I was able to focus on sketching my picture in order to relieve some of my stress. A few minutes later, I heard Aiden sit down in the seat next to me and say hello.

"Play it cool Nadia," I thought to myself.

I looked up to see him pulling his art supplies out of the bag and put them on the table.

"Hey Aiden," I said. "How was the rest of your weekend?"

"It was pretty good. Thanks for coming to the art exhibition with me on Saturday. I had a really good time," he said.

"Thanks again for inviting me," I replied.

"Oh! Before I forget, I have something to show you," said Aiden as he flipped through his sketchbook. "After you left, I was waiting for my mom to finish talking to her friends and I was able to sketch this."

Handing the paper to me, I looked to see the famous James Scott Fountain except the regal lions were replaced with cartoon ones playing in the fountain water. I laughed out loud at see the cartoon-like take on the fountain.

"This is great!" I exclaimed.

I really loved the drawing and its attention to detail on the animated faces of the lions. I went to hand the picture back to him and he scratched his head like he was nervous and immediately handed it back to me. I was a bit taken aback.

"You should use this for your portfolio," I said.

"Actually, I drew it for you," he mumbled under his breath.

"For me?" I replied in shock. "Are you sure?"

"Yeah, consider it a gift." He said smiling deeply.

I didn't know what to say to that. I had never been given a drawing for a gift. I usually drew things and gave them to other people. But I took the picture graciously and put it in my sketchbook so that it wouldn't get all crinkled up.

"Thank you for this; you didn't have to," I said shyly.

"I wanted to," he said.

I was speechless and even when I could drum up something intelligent to say in my babbling mind it was too late. Mr. Rider strolled into the classroom with a harried look upon his face.

"I'm sorry I'm late everyone, traffic was a mess. Who's ready to get drawing?" he asked.

Now into the third week of classes we had moved onto the lessons about how to tell a story which included everything from basic story structure to staging and cinematography. We were moving pretty quickly through the lessons since it was a summer course.

I found it hard to keep up at times, and I knew I wasn't the only student in the classroom that felt that way. Mr. Rider was trying to break everything down piece by piece, but I knew he sometimes felt that we were struggling with certain themes and concepts.

While this class didn't feature as much drawing as I thought it would, I still felt it was important that I got the fundamentals of animation down and not skip the steps of learning the basics.

At the beginning of the class, we would have a warm up sketch, then a lecture about whatever part of animation that we were currently working on and then break for lunch. After lunch we put the fundamentals into use by reviewing a piece of animation, and then broke it down piece by piece.

With every class I found that there was more stuff that I didn't know about animation and the hard work that was behind bringing beloved characters and stories to life. I had an even deeper appreciation for the cartoons I grew up watching as a kid. I was amazed and a bit intimidated and wondered if I was cut out to be an animator. Thankfully, next week was the fourth week and Mr. Rider would do review lessons covering everything we had learned so far.

The class was already halfway over and I couldn't believe it! Only three more weeks of lessons left! I made so many new friends and I was starting to see where my relationship with Aiden was headed. Maybe we'd continue to hang out even after the classes ended. Since he lived in the area, it wouldn't be too hard to meet up and hang out.

On the plus side, in just a couple of weeks, Mia would be back from Florida and we could start our annual summer bucket list. Why did summer vacation always have to go by so fast? It's like the saying goes, "time flies when you're having fun."

When it came time for lunch, instead of going outside with the others as we had been doing the past couple of weeks, I approached Mr. Rider with the hopes that he would take a look at the comic book project I had been working on.

"Hey Mr. Rider," would you mind if I could speak with you for a bit?" I asked.

"Sure, have a seat and let's talk," he replied.

I went over the comic book with him and showed him some of my artwork eager to hear some of his feedback. He carefully studied my storyboards and concept sketches with great care while flipping through my sketchbook in silence. This was probably the first time I had seen him looking so serious the whole time I had been in his class.

I knew that he was concentrating while I sat

there in nervous silence hoping for good feed-back about all of the hard work I had put into my creation.

"What would he think?" I thought to myself, "Would he like it or absolutely hate it?"

Finally, after some time passed and after jotting down some notes on a piece of paper, he began to speak.

"I remember sitting where you are on the other side of the desk many times as a young student and even as an intern. I know how important this is to you and I am proud that you had the courage to show me your work. That's the first step as an artist. I'll do my best to give you some constructive criticism, but don't take it the wrong way," he said.

For the first half of the lunch hour, I was so grateful that he took the time to go through my sketches and the art that I had drawn out so far. He pointed out parts of the story that could improve and other parts that needed very little changes. He thought my clumsy superhero idea was pretty clever and he praised me for it. In his words, it was wacky and fun.

"I think you're very talented and have a lot

of potential, Nadia. The best advice I can give you is to keep practicing and to always believe in your own ideas, no matter how crazy they might seem," he said.

He was even nice enough to give me some reference books I could use for further studying. I was so appreciative and hung on to all of his words and advice.

"Thank you so much Mr. Rider! This means a lot to me!" I said smiling.

"Anytime you need help, don't hesitate to come to me. You're usually a bit quieter in class, but don't be afraid to ask questions," said Mr. Rider, "We're not here to judge you, and we're all here to learn from each other."

Grabbing my sketchbook and other materials, I headed outside to eat lunch with everyone else. Usually everyone stayed to eat outdoors, but today there weren't as many people outside. Some of the older students who had cars must be out running errands. I looked around and saw Yoona, Linda, and Aiden waving me down to save a seat for me.

"So how'd it go?" everyone asked collectively.

"It actually went better than I thought it

would," I replied.

"I told you so," said Yoona, "It's all in your head. My cousin has taken some of Mr. Rider's animation courses before and she said that he was always one of the most easygoing teachers in the art department at her school."

"I guess I've just got to be more confident in my artwork," I said.

Chatting with everyone and their own personal experiences gave me feel better. I could tell that they were trying to make me feel reassured about the art critiquing process as a whole. Sometimes it was hard to hear, but it was something that you needed to do as an artist. My friends shared their ups and downs; their memories of winning art awards only to still be rejected from art programs. It was okay to be upset, but the most important thing was to not let it get to you.

While everyone else went inside into the classroom during the last part of our lunch break, Aiden and I were left sitting at the table alone.

"I can't believe how time has passed by so quickly," I said. "We only have three weeks left and then it's all over when it feels like it just started.

"I feel the same way," Aiden said, "Everyone feels like one big family here."

I nodded in agreement. It felt friendships were ending before they could truly begin. Luckily, most of the class lived in the area and we had talked about doing meetups after the class ended.

What Aiden said next would catch me off guard.

"I have wanted to ask you this since last Saturday, but would you go out with me?" he asked.

I did everything in my power to keep my mouth from gaping like a fish. I was happy nonetheless.

He continued blushing, but trying to play it cool, "I know we've hung out, but I'd like to go on a proper date and get to know you. You're beautiful and I feel as if I can always talk to you about anything. I'd really like to get to know you even more, if you'd let me."

I had felt even closer to him since last Saturday and I was hoping he would ask me out soon.

But to actually hear the words come from his mouth was jaw-dropping.

Even though I felt dancing with joy, I did my best to keep my emotions in check.

"I'd like to get to know you better too," I said smiling.

He smiled too. We exchanged numbers and talked for the rest of the lunch period. Once lunch was almost over he got up from the table to go back into the classroom. He paused, turning around to wait for me to walk with him.

"I'll be right there! I said, I just need to make a call," I said.

"See you inside," he replied.

As soon as he was out of sight, I did a little shimmy dance to celebrate. It was one of the happiest days of my teenage life!

I immediately texted Mia, telling her the good news making sure not to leave out any details. I knew she would be more than happy for me. I remembered she said that she and her family were out on a day trip, so I probably wouldn't hear back from her until later on, but when she did see my text I'd knew she'd be blowing up my phone with a hundred messages.

I sighed happily; maybe I just needed a little bit of romance to spice up my life.

As I headed back to the classroom, I was eager for a big announcement that Mr. Rider had alluded to the week before. I was hoping for a project that was challenging, but also fun too. As the rest of the class chatted among each other, you could feel the excitement buzz around the room.

While Aiden sat next to me, we began to chat up about the newest anime adaptation to come to the United States. Both of weren't that big of a big fan of these remakes as we felt like they just hoped they honored the original spirit of the film. While deep on conversation, Mr. Rider walked into the room with a big smile.

"We've got a lot to cover before classes, so let's begin," he stated.

"So before our class comes to an end in a few weeks, I'd like to do a special project where everyone could show off their skills and pays tribute to your favorite piece of animation. I want you all to apply the basics of animation and draw a character or theme that you will reinterpret in your own art style. I want you to spend the next 10 minutes coming up with which animation piece you like to work on. Your partner for this project will be your desk mate. And go!"

Immediately everyone got to work as soon as possible, swiveling around in their chairs and striking up a conversation of what to do. Aiden and I looked at each other and before we could say anything I knew what we both were thinking.

"Studio Ghibli!" we exclaimed out loud at the same time.

"But what film should we work on? *Spirited Away* is a beautiful film, but the animation is super detailed," I said thinking out loud.

"How about *My Neighbor Totoro*?" , asked Aiden.

"That would be fun! Totoro is easy to draw and we can switch up his character art too," I replied.

Once we made our decision, there was a few minutes left to pick an animation piece. Before we knew it, 10 minutes had passed.

Mr. Rider said "Time's up everyone!" He went around the room and talked to each desk and writing notes of what we would work on for the project. It was decided, Aiden and I would focus on the Studio Ghibli film *My Neighbor Totoro*, but both of us were a bit worried. The film studio was notable for its very detailed and picturesque art, so we hoped we could pay tribute to the film in a good way.

"Make sure you keep in contact with your project partner outside of class and communicate with each other. This is a group project, not a solo one so make sure you work together. I want you guys to get to know your classmates better through this project, but have fun too. I can't wait to see everyone's end results. If you ever have questions, I'm here to help," said Mr. Rider.

I couldn't wait to work on this project and spend more time with Aiden!

Later that night after dinner, I danced around my room to my favorite tunes. I wanted to work on my comic books but was restless so I needed to get up and move around. I couldn't sit still, no matter how hard I tried. All of sudden I heard my phone pinging multiple times in a row. The pings were so rapid in succession that it almost sounded like a little song. Before I looked at my phone I knew that had to be Mia. I opened my text messages to see:

Mia: *OMG*

Mia: *OMG. This is not a joke right? You're serious?! OMG.*

Mia: *\*sings\* Nadia's got a boyfriend! Nadia's got a boyfriend!*

Mia: *I need more details stat.*

Mia: *When? Where? Why? How?*

Mia: *Call me when you get this text!*

Mia: ☺

I looked though her messages and started laughing out loud. Before I could even call her, my phone rang and I looked at my caller ID to see Mia's face pop up on my screen. I answered the phone, and immediately heard happy squealing.

"Omg Nadia! I'm so happy for you!" she said. "From what you've told me, he sounds like a really great guy. Now I need to know everything that happened. Start from beginning to end."

I launched into the story of how we spent the day together on Saturday and how he casually asked me out on a formal date.

She sighed with envy, "Where's *my* dream prince? Question, does he have a hot brother or cousin that's single?"

"He does," I replied laughing, "But he might be a bit young for you. He's eight."

"Well there's always hope," she replied.

Turning the conversation back towards her, I asked all about her trip. Listening to her dramatic storytelling reenactments made me a bit sad. I was so glad she was coming back home in a week. I missed my best friend, and we already missed out on a good part of the summer not getting to hang out with each other. Hopefully, we would be able to finish some of our summer bucket list if not everything on it. We talked late into the night gabbing about everything.

I wasn't ready to go to sleep just yet, so I continued to sketch in my notebook and until I heard another ping from my phone. Looking down at my phone, I saw it was a text message from Aiden.

Instead of going to sleep we ended up texting for hours on end late into the rest of night and into the early morning. We talked about everything and anything until we fell asleep. I guess since we would be going on our first official date, that we were boyfriend and girlfriend now.

Maybe I was getting too ahead of myself? Or perhaps I was overthinking things as usual.

♦

## CHAPTER EIGHT

S UDDENLY, SATURDAY was here. I woke
up early since today I was meeting Aiden
at the Detroit Public Library. We wanted
some time outside of class to work together on
our project, plus this library has a wide variety
of Studio Ghibli animation books. Maybe we
could find something to help spark an idea.

As I arrived at the front entrance and walked
up the front steps, I looked up to see Aiden grinning at me with his big smile. In return I waved
back and waved a shy hello.

"Hey Aiden!" I said excitedly.

"Hey," he said in reply.

"Ready to get to work?" I nodded yes as we
walked through the front door.

Immediately I was in awe of the sights
before me. The ceilings were tall and lined with

detailed architecture designs and portraits that lined the halls. I couldn't help my jaw from dropping. Aiden must have seen the look of surprise on my face.

"It's pretty cool isn't it? This is one of my favorite places to visit," said Aiden. "I'll show you around first and then we can get started on our project. There is some artwork that you definitely have to see."

"Sounds great," I said.

We walked around the galleries and Aiden pointed out some of the art murals that lined the walls and statues that stood in hallways. This was the best library I had ever seen in all of my life. There were so many study rooms and books that lined the shelves! Even though the library was massive it still had a very cozy feeling to it. Once we finished walking around the library, we headed over to the reference desk to locate the books we needed for our project.

The woman at the reference gave us a map and pointed out sections where we could find the best art books for our project. We made our way over to the art section and looked for books on Ghibli movies and Japanese animation that we could use for reference. There weren't a ton of books to choose from, but at least we had each gathered up some online sources before we met so we had a lot of content to choose from. Once we gathered all of the books we thought we could use for our project we made our way to one of the open study tables and started to get to work.

Sitting with a table cluttered full of books and our laptops we got to work. We sat and flipped through books, while sketching out ideas.

"Since *My Neighbor Totoro* is centered around nature for most of the film, what if we took drawings of Totoro and placed him in local parks?" asked Aiden.

"That would be cool!" I replied, "And what if we used photographs of the parks for the background and drew everything else?," I said thinking out loud. "We can give the pictures a mixed media feel, kind of like the movie *Who Framed Roger Rabbit*?"

"I like how you're thinking," said Aiden nodding in agreement.

While we worked on sketches and finding

park photographs we wanted to use for our project we chatted about anything and everything. I learned more about Aiden and he shared stories of the places he grew up in. From visiting white sandy beaches to viewing some of the most unique museums, I was hooked into his stories. He seemed so adventurous and down to earth.

I shared stories from childhood, growing up in the area and sharing some local tips on how to find the best art hot spots. I didn't feel awkward or nervous at all.

Before I knew it, I looked at my cellphone and it was 5:00 PM. Where had the time gone? The library was closing soon so we started to pack up our items and to put the books back on cart to be re-shelved.

We had everything we needed, so it was just a matter of continuing to finish the concept art we had started on. We divided the pictures between us so that we had an equal amount of work to do. We decided to exchange email address so we could send each other the progress work and give feedback. Our project was going to be great!

The weeks blurred into one another and before I knew it, we were at the last week of the class. We had finished learning most of the fundamentals of animation at this point and were starting to review the basics. For the past couple of weeks Mr. Rider had us designing our own original characters and then create a comic strip using the storyboarding techniques he has showed us.

While I was happy, I was also sad at the same time. This was the experience of a lifetime getting to learn about the art of animation and it truly did help me understand the basics more than I thought I knew. I had had so many memories packed into such a short time and I hoped that I would be lucky enough to take another one of Mr. Rider's classes in the future. He was an art teacher that would leave a long-lasting impression on my life. Hopefully, what I learned in this class would help me for years to come in the future.

As the rest of the students got ready for class, it felt a bit somber in the room as well. I could tell that Mr. Rider picked up on it as he walked into the class and got ready for the day's session.

"Why the long faces everyone?" he said surveying the room. "Look, I know our time together was short but we've had so much fun. I've enjoyed getting to meet each and every one of you also. Let's try to make the best of this last week and create good memories."

Mr. Rider's motivational speech was successful in perking up everyone's mood as we got to work.

Aiden and I smiled at each other and then we pulled out our sketchbook and got to work as class begun. For the last week, we got to review the basics of animation and point out the specific techniques in popular media. It was his way of testing us and make sure that we had understood everything we were learning.

In between that time, we were all still working on our final project of using TV or film animation, then applying that to our own drawings of a character or theme that we would create in our own art style. We had been working on the project for a couple of weeks in between lectures, and each table had been hard at work finalizing our project. Aiden and I had almost finished up the project, but still had some final touches to work on.

Though we took a lunch break, everyone continued working on sketches outdoors while eating. This was a huge project and it was time-consuming. Plus everyone wanted to show off their art skills and to prove they had what it takes in this class to succeed. Because of this, lunch was a bit quieter than usual but we still chatted while reminiscing about our favorite moments of the class.

We had all agreed on putting together a reunion meetup of sorts at a local art museum and restaurant so that everyone could hang out with one another this summer. We all worked on putting together our schedules and decided we would meet up on a Saturday next month. I was looking forward to be able to hang out with everyone.

We continued working hard our on our projects until Thursday when it was time for our presentation. During the presentations, everyone was a bit nervous but we took our time as one by one we presented our art projects to the class. Everyone's work was so impressive and I couldn't believe all of the interesting ideas they came up with.

Aiden and I did a great job on our presentation. Not only did we have more time to spend with each other, but we able to bounce ideas off one another. We were a great project team.

Presenting our work to the class, I felt happy and proud of my work. Instead trying to recreate the work or try to blend in with the study of the original artwork, we infused the images from the movie in reference to local places that mirrored memorable parts of the movie. We got a lot of compliments from everyone else!

After everyone was finished, Mr. Rider surprised the class with various kinds of pizzas for lunch and while we were munching on food he got up from his desk to speak.

"I'm so proud of each and every one of you. Thank you for allowing me to teach you and for you to teach me in return. Everyone is so talented here, and I hope by continuing to draw that I'll see more of your works someday soon. I hope I get the chance to speak with you all again in the future. Please keep in touch," he said.

Once our final class came to an end, we lingered longer than usual. People hugged each other as we said our goodbyes. I would miss this class so much! Aiden and I set up for our first date at the Detroit Riverwalk in the next couple of weeks, and we hugged as we said goodbye.

Once I got home, I relaxed and ate dinner with my parents while we watched our favorite movies like *Jurassic Park*. I got a text notification from Mia on my phone and we made plans to hang out next weekend since she was coming back home this weekend. I knew she probably wanted some time to get settled in and recuperate from her month away from home and also some time to unpack. I couldn't wait to hang out again since it seemed that summer was going by way too fast.

●

# LOST LOVE: MY FIRST BOYFRIEND

## CHAPTER NINE

S INCE MIA was back from her vacation,
we made plans to hang out. She wanted
to meet Aiden in person as well, but we
decided to hang out with just the two of us
in order to catch up on girl chat. We decided
upon going to Belle Isle to cross off two of our
summer bucket list items on our list: visiting
Belle Isle and going to the beach. Though Belle
Isle had a small beach it was the one that was
closest to us.

Packing up all my beach gear, I decided to
pack a picnic basket full of food as well. As I was
cutting up food in the kitchen to pack, my mom
popped her head in the kitchen and asked if I
was almost ready to go.

My mom and Mia's mom, Mrs. Lopez, would
be joining us for an all-out girl's day. They took

some time off at work since they had been very busy and wanted to spend some time with us as well. After finishing packing up the picnic basket, we hopped in the car and went on our way to the park.

The air was warm, but somewhat breezy. I was glad it wouldn't be too hot, but if the weather decided to change its mind I prepared by bringing mini fans, water, and lots of sunscreen. When we finally got to the park, it took some time to find parking near the beach area. Apparently everyone else had the same idea to go to the beach today too.

We unloaded the car and looked around for Mia and her mom among the crowd of beach-goers. Walking around, we found them near the water park under a giant umbrella and beach blankets. Mia and I swapped stories of our how our summers were going so far and got caught up with one another.

After soaking up some of the sun, we left our mothers to go to the water park to try out some of the newest slides. We slid down the gigantic slides in inflatable tubes, racing through the rapid waters of the tunnels. We got soaked, but we had a blast! After we started to get hungry, we headed back to our spot on the beach.

I dug some food out of the picnic basket and, to my surprise, my mom had picked up some street tacos from one of the food trucks parked nearby. While munching on food, Mia showed me some of her Florida vacation pictures. She showed me her grandparents' house, the white sandy beaches, and even some pictures from their impromptu trip to the Magic Kingdom at Disney World. She also shared tons of stories from her family reunion. Mia then ran over to her bag and pulled out a small gift bag.

"Here's a little souvenir for you," she said.

Opening the bag eagerly, I saw it was a stuffed plushy of the green alien from the *Toy Story* movie.

"How cute!" I exclaimed. "Thanks so much bestie!" I said, giving her a hug.

The four of us spent the rest of the day relaxing, chatting, and playing games on the beach. Before we knew it, the sun started to set and it was time to go. We started to pack up our items along with other beachgoers and then said goodbye.

"I'll text you later or tomorrow," said Mia, "And we'll figure out the next thing to tackle on our summer bucket list."

I nodded in agreement and waved as her mom and she walked away. Once we were in the car, we drove home enjoying the city's sights in silence. Exhausted and finally at home after a long day, we couldn't wait to shower and hit the sack.

◊ ◊ ◊

A couple of weeks passed, and it was finally time for me and Aiden's first date!

I was nervous and excited for what the day would bring. I tossed and turned all night long since I was so anxious. I asked what we would be doing for the day, but Aiden said it was a surprise. He told me to meet him in Hart Plaza by noon.

I got up early in the morning trying to tame my frizzy hair since the humidity of the summer weather was making it hard to tame. After many attempts I managed to make a cute side bun and then it was time to find an outfit to wear. I spent an hour agonizing over what to wear and finally decided on a purple summer floral dress. I wanted to dress up, but still be casual at the same time.

When I met Aiden at Hart Plaza, he surprised me with a picnic basket and we found a place to sit near the waterfront off of the Detroit River. It was a beautiful, sunny day. There were lots of people out walking their dogs, jogging, and relaxing outdoors. He set up the blanket on the grass and set out a variety of foods for us to eat. Everything looked delicious.

Embarrassingly enough, my stomach decided to growl loudly since I didn't eat breakfast that morning. His head popped up from setting up our plates and we both made eye contact. After a few moments of silence, we both started laughing.

"What a way to start a date, Nadia," I thought, groaning internally.

The picnic was so romantic and it felt like something out of a fairytale. We ate and talked about everything from hobbies to art.

"So what kind of art would you like to in the future," he asked.

I pondered the question for a bit.

"Well, I think I'd like to work in Japanese animation field. I wouldn't mind working here in the United States or working abroad in Japan. I love their animation process, and I think if I can practice enough, I'll have a chance," I replied. "What about you?" I asked.

"I think I'd like to work on graphic novels. I love to draw, but I love to write even more. So maybe publishing is more of my career route," he replied.

We continued to talk about art and then after eating we decided to get up and walk around.

We found some bikes to rent as there were various MoGo Bike Rental stations around the Downtown area. We rode through the parks and on Riverwalk admiring the river views and enjoying the cool breeze as we whisked by. It had gotten pretty hot by this time and so the cool wind was much appreciated.

Taking a break, we found some ice cream to purchase at the snack bar and then sat next to each other on a bench enjoying each other's company. We then decided to ride through Dequindre Cut Greenway admiring all of the cool graffiti art murals that lined the walls while racing each other to the end.

Soon the date was coming to an end and before we parted ways, he asked me officially to be his girlfriend!

On the car ride home until the entire time I went to bed I was smiling from ear to ear. This was one of the best days. I had in a long time.

◊ ◊ ◊

Our second date was spent going to a local arcade which was fun for both of us. It felt like we were little kids again and we raced up and down along the game aisles to see what we wanted to play next. We goofed off while holding multiple dance-off challenges in *Dance Dance Revolution*, raced each other in *Mario Kart*, and shot hoops at the basketball games. This date brought out our playful sides and it felt nice to let loose more than usual.

Even when we weren't meeting up to go on dates, we talked almost every day and even did drawing sessions via Skype. Since we're both preparing for high school, we got busier as the summer went on, so it was harder to meet up since we were in art class together. I hung out with Mia, helped my parents continue the rest of "project cleanup" by tidying the rest of the house, and continued to work on my own art projects.

Aiden and I still made an effort to meet each other for coffee when we could spare some time and did our best to keep the spark alive. The more time we had spent with each other, the more we fell in love. Though we had only met a little over a month ago, I felt so close to Aiden. He knew how to always make me laugh and smile and I loved that about his personality. Our relationship continued to grow even though we couldn't always spend time together in a traditional way.

Heading into the latter part of the summer, our art class group met at the Detroit Institute of Arts. It is one of the world's most notable art museums and has one of the largest and most significant art collections in the United States.

We were there to not only meet up as a group, but to check out their newest exhibit "The Art of Animation." The exhibit displayed different types of animation from all over the world as well as the behind the scenes views of famous cartoons.

Since we bought the tickets that day, we had to wait until our scheduled time slot allowed us to enter the exhibit. We had some time to kill, so we made our way through galleries while admiring the stunning architecture of the building. Everyone was in awe of the art, especially the gigantic Diego Rivera mural in the Rivera Court.

Aiden and I hung towards the back of the group and walked together hand and hand. Every so often I would see my classmates wiggling their eyebrows at us, winking, or throwing heart signs at us.

Linda was the least surprised to see us together as a couple. She said, "A mom always knows these things."

To make things more fun we played a game of "I Spy" in each room.

It was finally our turn into the animation exhibit and everyone was pointing out their favorite films and cartoons. They even had a ton of short films from independent film companies playing in the background. We were able to point out a lot of fundamental principles of animation that we had spent learning in our class.

While we walked through the exhibit, I kept sneaking glances at Aiden from the side. I noticed that he was more quiet that usual. When he would catch my eye, he would smile and then look off in the distance.

I couldn't exactly put my finger on it, but he seemed bothered about something. When I finally asked what was wrong he shrugged it off as nothing. Though we enjoyed ourselves at the museum, I couldn't help but feel that Aiden seemed a bit distant from the rest of the group.

Though we felt very comfortable with one another, I was slightly upset that he wasn't sharing what was on his mind with me. We shared everything with each other; he was my best friend and boyfriend too. I decided to let it go, but not without his behavior leaving a slightly nagging feeling during the rest of our time spent at the museum.

Afterwards, we went to a nearby Italian restaurant to eat. Everyone swapped stories about their summers and even funny stories from the times that we shared together in class. We laughed non-stop throughout dinner and even played game of Pictionary drawing on our napkins. Luckily, we were able to get a table at the back of the restaurant so we didn't disturb any of the other customers enjoying their dinner.

It was such a fun day, and I was sad to see it end. I looked forward to the next meetup that we had planned in the near future.

◆

# LOST LOVE: MY FIRST BOYFRIEND

## CHAPTER TEN

TODAY WAS the big day I was waiting for! It was the day of the festival that was the highlight of the summer that everyone looked forward to.

Hopefully it would cheer Aiden up because I noticed he still seemed more and more distracted as time went by. I was hoping to be able to get to the bottom of things and figure out why he seemed so down. I looked outside of my bedroom window to see the sun shining brightly in the sky. I kept checking the weather forecast the whole week long wishing and praying that the forecast wouldn't change.

I went over to my closet to find my most fitting festival clothes. I knew I would be walking around a lot and that the festival was located on fairgrounds with dusty roads so maybe a frilly outfit would not be a good idea. Finally settling on jean capris, a colorful T-shirt, hoodie, and tennis shoes I was satisfied. Getting ready in the bathroom I sang the whole time through my morning routine. I felt refreshed, energetic, and ready for the day.

Running downstairs I was greeted by my parents watching TV in the living room. They weren't partial to crowds so they decided to skip out on the festival this year. Secretly though, I think it was just to give Aiden and me some space.

I ate my breakfast and scrolled through Instagram to see the latest artist challenge to go viral. Once I had some more concrete sketches, I decided that I would create my own artist Instagram profile and start sharing my art with others.

As I finished eating, I heard a car horn honk outside. I received a text notification from Mia saying, "We're here!"

Once I cleaned up my dishes I said goodbye to my parents and raced out the door.

Opening the door to get into the car, I greeted Mia enthusiastically. Once I was buckled in, we were off to the fairgrounds.

"Are you excited for today?," Mia asked, "We're going to have so much fun and then later on you can meet up with your boo."

I laughed and rolled my eyes. Mia's sense of humor and her kind heart were just two of the greatest things about being her friend.

At least we would get to cross off yet another thing on our Summer Bucket List: "eat a funnel cake at the local fair." It was going to be a good day. And I got to spend it with my best friend and my boyfriend.

Once we arrived at the fairgrounds we were greeted by all the sights and the sounds of the fair. There were carnival games, rides, an art show, animals, and lots of food trucks to go around. Mia's mom was helping to run one of the exhibition booths for her workplace.

"If you guys need me, just call or text my phone anytime," said Mrs. Lopez, "Have fun girls!"

We waved goodbye and decided to walk around to see what there was to do. Aiden wouldn't arrive until later, so we had plenty of time to hang out. After walking through the fairgrounds, we decided to start with a few rides. We rode on all the classic rides like the Tilt-A-Whirl and the Pirate Ship, smiling, screaming, and laughing as the wind whipped our hair around in a frenzied manner. For us, the more thrilling a ride was, the better!

Wanting to take a break after the rides, we headed over the to the food court. There were so many food trucks to choose from! My eyes glazed over at all the food choices. Festival food was so tasty, so it was hard to narrow down our choices. Mia and I pondered over our options and ordered some Butterfly Chips; thin, home-made potato chips covered in cheese, sour cream, chives, and bacon. To wash it all down, we each got a fruit smoothie at a nearby booth and then headed over to the dessert section while letting some of our food digest. We bought a funnel cake to share and then walked around to the art show area to check out the feature artists.

Looking at all the artists' pieces, I was in awe. Hopefully, my art would be good enough to display up there too one day in the future. After we finished looking at the art show, we rode a couple of more rides and then sat down on the bench to relax a bit more and people watch. I heard my phone ping with a new text notification and I saw that Aiden had texted.

Aiden: *Sorry I'm a bit late, but I'm here. Where are you?*

Me: *Mia and I are sitting next to the rides area, near the roller coaster. You can't miss it.*

Aiden: *I'm on my way.* ☺

Me: ☺

I smiled from ear to ear, while texting. Mia glanced over and saw my face.

"Well, I guess this is my cue to leave. Aiden's here isn't he?" she asked.

I nodded excitedly.

"Are you sure you don't want to hang with us?" I asked.

"I don't want to be a third wheel. Plus you two need to go and be lovebirds," Mia said while wiggling her eyebrows and mischievously grinning. "I'll see you two later. I'll be at my mom's work booth if you need me," she said and waved as she walked away.

Not a minute later, Aiden walked into my view.

"Hey," he said a bit flustered. "Sorry I'm so late."

"It's no problem, what would like to do first?" I asked.

"Let's grab a bite to eat," he said, and we walked hand in hand.

Even though I had eaten earlier in the day with Mia, I found myself hungry for more food. We decided on buying some Coney dogs to eat. While waiting for our food to be ready we danced along to the music that was playing in the background.

After we got our food, we found an open table in the picnic area and sat down to eat. He was quieter than usual and seemed a bit reluctant to engage in conversation. I didn't want to pry, but it seemed like something that was deeply worrying him.

After eating, we decided to head to the rides area.

"What would you like to go on?" Aiden asked.

"You pick," I said smiling at him.

I could never get tired of looking at his cute dimples.

We headed for the Scrambler and laughed as we flew around in the air. We went on a couple of other rides nearby and looked around for other things to do.

Walking and holding hands, we decided to go on the love boat ride. It was quiet, peaceful, and relaxing as we rode along in the boat. When I was with Aiden, I always felt so comfortable. I laid my head on his shoulder and we sat in silence as we gazed at the sights and sounds of the ride.

After the boat ride ended, Aiden went to the bathroom and then came back with a large cotton candy to surprise me. I was so touched by the gesture. He remembered that I loved cotton candy. This is what I loved about Aiden; he was so thoughtful and kind.

As we finished the cotton candy, he suggested that we should ride on the Ferris wheel next. After getting settled into our cart we were whisked into the sky with breathtaking views of the festival below.

The sun was starting to set for the evening and its afterglow cast an illuminating effect on the entire fairgrounds. We looked out into the view and then back at each other as we gazed into each other's eyes.

We spent the rest of the ride snuggled up together while holding hands. When I went to put my head on his shoulder this time around, he seemed to hesitate. He sat me up straight and looked into my eyes.

"Nadia, I have something to tell you," he said seriously.

Maybe he was finally getting off his chest what's been bothering him lately.

"I'm going away," he said.

That was it? I thought.

"Oh. Where to? When are you coming back?" I said.

He hesitated once again. "I mean... we're moving away," he continued.

I said nothing.

"My dad just got a new job offer and we're moving to Seattle before the summer ends."

I was speechless.

"When were you going to tell me?" I said after some moments.

"Well, my dad mentioned something about a few weeks ago, but nothing was confirmed until today."

My eyes started to water and filled up with tears as we got off of the ride and walked down the midway. I didn't turn around and kept walking forward without looking at him.

I was so hurt and heartbroken. I couldn't believe that as soon as I met him, he was already going away before my very eyes.

He put his hand on my shoulder and slowly turned around. Looking at his face I saw that he was so sad.

"I didn't want to have to do this to you, but I don't have a choice," he said sadly.

"Will you come back to visit at all?" I asked in hopeful anticipation he would say yes.

"I'll try to convince my parents, but I can't guarantee it."

"Well I guess this is goodbye then," I said.

Before he could say anything further I dashed away and back to the booths where Mia and her Mom were.

Tears flowed freely as I couldn't contain my emotions anymore. I needed my best friend. Mia took one look at me when she saw me and pulled me into a giant hug. No words were said, just by looking at my face she knew what was wrong. Mia and her mom did the best to console me on the way back home, but I just sat in silence looking out the window.

Once I got home, I greeted my parents, walked up stairs to the bathroom and took a long hot shower to help calm myself. Then after I got ready for bed I finally lay down and stared at the ceiling in sorrow. The summer memories all flashed before me: meeting Aiden, sharing lunch during art class, our trip to Belle Isle Park, first date, and all of the other special moments we had shared together. While the summer got off to a great start, it ended badly.

◊ ◊ ◊

I spent the first week after the breakup in a daze. I was sad, moody, and full of hurt. I marathoned my favorite animation films to help to lift my spirts. I also spent a lot of time in my family's garden trying to ease the worries in my mind. Somewhere in the back of my mind I wondered how Aiden was doing, but I turned my focus mainly on healing my heart.

As the weeks went on the pain in my heart

slowly eased and I pushed myself to enjoy the last remains of summer vacation. I worked on finishing up my first draft of my comic book, finding drawing as a way to cope. I spent lots of time with Mia and hung out more with my friends from art class too. We went around the neighborhood and check out some of local fairs that were happening.

In the midst of my free time I started to prep for high school. My parents helped me pick out some of the supplies I needed for school. I was very excited for my school's art program since I heard such good things about it. Yoona, from my summer art class, was going into sophomore year at my high school. I was glad that I would know another friendly face at my new school.

When I initially met up with my art class friends they were so shocked at the breakup between Aiden and I. They understood the circumstances, and were very supportive of me. They were a great source of support for me when the breakup first happened and continued to be solid friends.

They did give me updates about Aiden. He had tried to text me an apology to me many times by texting me, but I wasn't having it. I wanted a better explanation and I wanted an apology face-to-face. My friends told me that Aiden had felt regret for how things ended and wanted to make up things badly.

◊ ◊ ◊

Today, I was meeting up with Aiden for the last time.

We had talked a few times by phone, but I wanted to meet up with him in person to confront him. When we did talk he kept apologizing over and over again. He seemed so sad about his upcoming move and I could hear the emotion in his voice.

He told me he had spent most of the rest of the summer helping his family pack up all their stuff to prepare for the big move. His family was not too excited about having to move again, but ultimately accepted that they would look forward to the future and start new beginnings.

We decided to meet up at our local downtown shopping area where we met at the Java Café Coffee Shop. It was awkward between the two of us once we did meet. A heavy silence filled the air, and for a long time we said nothing to each other.

We didn't make eye contact and put all of our focus on the steaming cups of coffee that sat on the table before us. I tried to keep my emotions in check, but was failing miserably as my eyes became watery. I was hurt, angry, confused, and sad most of all. I spoke first.

"Why?" I asked, "I just want to know why. We spent all that time together and you had so many opportunities to tell me, but you never said a word. All this time I asked if something was wrong and you would never say anything?"

"I just didn't want to lose what we had," Aiden said looking at me. "I was mad at my dad for promising that we wouldn't have to move again and then changing plans as usual." he said.

"You could have talked to me about it though," I looked up at him. "That's no excuse for lying like that. I don't want to hear any more excuses from you," I said, looking back down in the coffee mug and seeing my sad reflection in the cup.

Tears started to roll from my eyes. I had nothing else to say.

He said nothing else. And then left a piece of paper on the table before getting up and walking out of the café.

I finally looked up wiping the tears from my face and saw a final gift. It was a sketch of our favorite place in town, the Starry Night Craft Shop where we had first met by coincidence.

◊ ◊ ◊

Looking back over the summer as the new school year started, all of the positives still outweighed the negatives. I had to choose to focus on the good things that happened to me in order to cope with my broken heart. And I could tell that new beginnings were on their way.

Maybe I would meet someone new, but for right now I had my friends and family by my side.

I wouldn't regret a single thing that happened the summer I lost my first boyfriend.

◆